Published by Creative Education
123 South Broad Street, Mankato, Minnesota 56001
Creative Education is an imprint of The Creative Company

Design and production by Stephanie Blumenthal
Printed in the United States of America

Photographs by Robert E. Barber, Corbis (Galen Rowell), Dennis Frates, Don Geyer, The Image Finders (Kenny Bahr,
Jim Baron, Gary Leppart, William Manning), JLM Visuals (Charlie Crangle, Robert Gernant, Helga & Ken Heiman,
Richard P. Jacobs, Lowell R. Laudon, John Minnich), KAC Productions (Bill Draker), John Perryman, George Robbins,
Tom Stack & Associates (Sharon Gerig, John Gerlach, Thomas Kitchin, Joanne Lotter, Allen B. Smith, Doug Sokell,
T. Stack, Spencer Swanger)

Library of Congress Cataloging-in-Publication Data

Bodden, Valerie.
Mountains / by Valerie Bodden.
p. cm. — (Our world)
Includes index.
ISBN-13 : 978-1-58341-463-7
1. Mountains—Juvenile literature. I. Title. II. Series.
QH87.B63 2006   551.43—dc22   2005053720

First Edition
2 4 6 8 9 7 5 3 1

OUR WORLD

MOUNTAINS

Valerie Bodden

Mountains are very big hills. They reach high up into the sky. Mountains are found all over the world. The highest mountain in the world is called Mount Everest. It stands almost six miles (10 km) high! Mount Everest is close to China.

Not all mountains look the same. Some mountains are pointy. Others are rounded. Some mountains have a hole in the top! They are called **volcanoes**.

There are many kinds of mountains

The tops of most mountains are covered with rock. It can be very cold on top of a mountain. There is snow on top of some mountains. It can snow a lot on top of a mountain. It can even snow in the summer!

The snow on some mountains is very deep

Plants grow at the bottom of many mountains. Trees grow at the bottom of some mountains. Some of the trees are big. Others are small. Flowers grow at the bottom of some mountains, too. Most of the flowers are bright colors. Many are purple, red, or yellow.

Flowers can make mountains colorful

All kinds of big animals live on mountains. Bears live on mountains. So do mountain goats. You can see deer on mountains. Bighorn sheep live there, too.

Some animals live up high

Small animals live on mountains, too. Squirrels and mice are small. They live on mountains. So do **insects** and spiders.

Animals find food to eat on mountains

Lots of birds live on mountains. Crows are birds. They live on mountains. Eagles and hawks are big birds. They live on mountains, too.

Birds live in the trees on some mountains

*Sheep and cows eat
the grass
on mountains*

Some people live on mountains. They build houses there. They drive up long roads to get to their houses. Lots of farmers let their cows **graze** at the bottom of mountains. Some farmers grow **crops** at the bottom of mountains.

Lots of people like to visit mountains. Some people camp on mountains. Others ski down the snow on mountains. Some people even climb mountains. People can have lots of fun on mountains!

There are lakes on some mountains

Over time, mountains get worn away. Wind wears mountains away. So does water. You can wear away your own mountain. Make a pile of dirt outside. Blow on your "mountain" through a straw. Then pour some water on top of the mountain. What happens to the dirt?

GLOSSARY

crops—plants that farmers grow in fields

graze—eat the plants in an area

insects—bugs that have six legs

volcanoes—mountains that melted rock can come out of

LEARN MORE ABOUT MOUNTAINS

Everest for Kids
http://www.alanarnette.com/
kids/everest10.htm

Rocky Mountain Photography
http://www.hanselmann
photography.com/INFO%20P
AGES/Imagaes.html

Rocky Mountain Wildlife for Kids
http://www.montrose.net/
wildlife/Kids/index.htm